GRIEVANCE IN GINGERBREAD ALLEY

LEIGHANN DOBBS

LEIGHANN DOBBS PUBLISHING

SUMMARY

When Augusta "Gus" Chance takes a break from her
duties as Sheriff of Mystic Notch to indulge in her
hobby of playing jazz piano in Christmas Village, she
never imagines that a surprise from her past will cause
her to become embroiled in the investigation of a suspicious death.

She soon discovers that Christmas Village isn't the
idyllic holiday retreat that it appears to be. Something
sinister is lurking beneath all that Christmas cheer, and
the village regulars are harboring dangerous secrets.

What does the murder have to do with the maids a-
milking, the swans a-swimming, and the partridge in

the pear tree? Gus is on a mission to find out, but she soon discovers that solving a murder is not so easy when you don't have the benefit of a sheriff's badge.

CHAPTER 1

Gus Chance hurried through the snow-covered streets of Christmas Village, humming a little tune and clutching her jazz sheet music to her chest. She wanted to get back to the small apartment above the cider store that she'd rented for the week so she could go over the music she would play later that night. Gus, a sheriff in the town of Mystic Notch, was on vacation in Christmas Village, and part of that vacation entailed pursuing her passion of playing jazz on the piano.

She'd secured a gig at a trendy little club called the North Pole Lounge and had even connected online with a sax player who could accompany her. The woman had good credentials and was, in fact, employed as one of the pipers piping in the village. Since Gus had never met her, they'd arranged to meet at the lounge before the gig to get acquainted with each other's playing styles. They'd picked out a few songs, and Gus had bought the sheet music. She wanted to be sure she was well acquainted with them before the gig.

Gus had only been in town a few days, but she already knew all the shortcuts. Knowing all the entrances and exits was part of her training as a sheriff, and she couldn't turn that off even when she was on vacation. The first thing she'd done when getting to town was stroll the streets and take note of where everything was.

Gus wasn't one hundred percent sure this village suited her. Oh, it was quaint, she'd give it that, but all the forced joy grated on her. She sensed an odd under-current. But that was Gus's way and one of the reasons why she was a good sheriff. She didn't see things the way others did. Where others saw pretty icicles, Gus saw frozen weapons that could fall and stab you like a sword. To Gus, the sparkly garlands wrapped around all the pine trees in town could be used to strangle some-one. And she didn't even want to get started on the twinkling lights over by the skating pond. Could you say electrocution?

Not to mention the snowmen with their glassy coal eyes and colorful scarves that seemed to pop up everywhere. She wasn't sure who made them but thought it was possibly someone in the chamber of commerce. Or maybe they just appeared. The children seemed delighted with them, but every time Gus walked past one, she felt like it was watching her.

Deep in thought, she started across the street only to jump back as a horse-drawn sleigh nearly ran her down. The horses snorted puffs of air, their hooves clomping on the street, bells jangling. Happy tourists sat in the back, holding mugs of hot cocoa. Yes, it was all very picturesque until you thought about what those horses must leave behind. Someone must be kept quite busy cleaning up the mess on the streets.

Glancing down the street to make sure nothing else was coming, she noticed the sign to the chocolate store. Hadn't she heard something about an elf being murdered behind there? Too bad she'd also heard it had been solved.

Just as well, she thought as she crossed the street and headed toward Gingerbread Alley, a shortcut to her cottage that was on the next street over. She was here to play the piano, not solve murders. She had plenty of that back home in Mystic Notch, where the murder rate seemed to have risen considerably since her sister, Willa, had moved to town.

Gus slipped into the alley, intending to hurry through to the street where her apartment was.

Unfortunately, a large crowd blocked the way.

"Save the birds!" A woman with bushy red hair tacked a flyer onto a pole. Gus had seen the flyers around town. They were for some sort of protest about the treatment of the birds that acted as tourist attractions in Christmas Village. A crowd had gathered around the woman.

"Why do the birds need to be saved?" a gray-haired woman in a brown wool coat and matching hat asked.

"The birds of Christmas Village are mistreated. Made to stay out in the cold and the snow. We must save them!" The bushy-haired woman sounded quite dedicated to her cause.

"They're not mistreated!" a younger woman with short blonde hair that spiked up on top of her head yelled from the edge of the crowd. "We take great care of our birds! They're treated like royalty. You know that, Vicky."

The bushy-haired woman, Vicky, narrowed her gaze on the blonde and waved her hand around. "This is not the normal environment for these birds. They're shivering."

"The birds are an integral part of Christmas Village!" said a short woman holding a box of chocolates covered in gold foil. "If you ship out the birds, it will affect tourism."

Vicky put her hands on her hips. "Tourism? Is that all you're worried about? The money? Well, I…"

The chocolate-bearing woman's face turned red, and she stuttered. "I… ack…"

"What?" the blonde persisted. "We have heated nests and everything."

Vicky's eyes practically bulged as she pointed at the blonde. "You…. Arghh…."

Then her eyes rolled up in her head, and she toppled onto her face, landing in the dusting of snow that always seemed to cover the ground in Christmas Village.

The crowd gasped and shuffled forward.

"Give her air!"

Instinctively, Gus pushed through the crowd toward the woman, her sheriff training taking over. "Step aside. Police."

She heard murmurs of heart attack or stroke.

She even thought she heard someone say, "Good riddance."

The woman lay face down, not moving a muscle.

This did not look good. Gus squatted beside her and pressed a finger to her carotid artery. No pulse.

She turned the body slightly so she could look at Vicky's face. The woman's eyes were partially open, and a little bit of foam gathered at the corner of her mouth. Someone was calling the ambulance, but Gus knew it was too late.

A wave of sadness swept over her as she realized her thoughts about Christmas Village not being the joyful place it pretended to be might be correct. Not only was the woman dead, but Gus suspected she'd been murdered.

"What're you doing? Let go of that body! You're tampering with a crime scene!"

The familiar voice was like a jolt of electricity straight to Gus's heart. She looked up to see the last person in the world she expected to find in Christmas Village: her old nemesis and instructor from the police academy, Detective Kristine Winters.

"You! What are *you* doing here?" Winters scowled down at Gus, making her feel like she was still a rookie cadet who couldn't do anything right. But she wasn't a rookie anymore. She was a sheriff with an impressive record. She took a deep breath and stood.

Fifteen years had passed since Gus had last seen her old teacher, and the woman had aged quite a bit. Her hair was snowy white, she wore reading glasses, and her belly was round. *Probably not much to do up here in Christmas Village except eat*, Gus thought. Gus glanced back at the body. Well, there was not much to do until now.

"I'm here on vacation." Gus brushed the snow off her pants.

"And messing around with dead bodies like you're not supposed to be." Winters's blue eyes flicked over to the body, then she directed her gaze to the crowd. "What happened here?"

"She just keeled over," an elf with curly-toed shoes said.

"My guess is she had a heart attack or stroke. She was pretty worked up," said a middle-aged man who Gus recognized as the man who ran the fruitcake shop.

"So, it looks like natural causes." Winters nodded at the detective who had accompanied her, a thin man in his late thirties. "What do you think, Detective Noel?"

Gus looked down at the body. She estimated the woman to have been in her early forties. Her purple lips and the foam on one corner of her mouth seemed to indicate she was poisoned. "I don't think so."

Winters's gaze snapped back to Gus. "Well, you're not the law enforcement here, are you?"

Gus squared her shoulders. She wasn't about to let Winters intimidate her, and she certainly wouldn't stand by and let a murder be labeled as natural causes. "No, but I *am* law enforcement in Mystic Notch, New Hampshire."

"Oh really? So you got a job finally?"

Gus ignored the barb. "Yes, I'm a sheriff." Gus pointed to her badge—or where her badge would've been if she was wearing her uniform.

Detective Noel cleared his throat. "Um… the medical examiner is here."

"Right, let him through, then," Winters said. She turned to Gus. "Let's not forget that I'm the law here. This death was likely just natural causes, but even so, I'll advise you to stay out of this. This is my crime scene, and I don't need a flunky rookie messing it up."

Gus stepped back and fought the tidal wave of anger rising inside her. She knew better than to argue with Winters. Why was she acting this way? Back when she was in the academy, Winters had been tough, but she'd been a good cop. Winters had pushed all of them pretty hard, but she'd pushed Gus in particular because Gus had messed up on her first case.

Well, she wasn't going to mess up this time.

As she faded back into the crowd, Gus scanned the crime scene. Because that was what she thought it was now—a crime scene. She was sure Vicky had been poisoned, and it was clear the woman made some enemies with this bird-saving crusade.

Some of the crowd had dispersed. Others were whispering. Gus caught snatches of conversation, but one in particular got her attention.

"The gals over at Ruffled Feathers will be happy she's gone. I heard their permit was in jeopardy because of all the squawking Vicky was doing."

Gus made a mental note to visit Ruffled Feathers as she looked for clues. The victim's purse had fallen over, and the contents were scattered about. Her appointment book had fallen open. Gus craned her neck. She just managed to see something written on today's date a second before Winters snatched the appointment book up and dropped it in an evidence bag. Gus had only gotten a quick look, but she thought she'd seen *perm meetg. st nic.*

At least the evidence bag was a good sign. Winters must be treating this like a crime, or she wouldn't be collecting evidence.

Was the meeting relevant? Had she already met the person, or was that for later? If the meeting had already taken place, maybe the person she'd met with didn't like what Vicky had to say. If it was for later, maybe someone didn't want that meeting to take place. But who was *st nic*? Gus almost snorted at the shorthand for Saint Nick. Maybe that wasn't so strange given they were in Christmas Village.

As she was thinking about how to learn more about the meeting, a man came rushing down the street.

"Vicky! No!" He fell to the ground beside the body, much to the dismay of the medical examiner, who was trying to work on it.

Winters gently tugged the man away, and he stumbled around the crime scene for a few minutes. "Sit down, Steve. There's nothing you can do."

"But she was fine this morning!" Steve started wailing.

Must be the husband. He seemed very upset, maybe *too* upset. Gus noticed he clutched a white takeout bag with a blue fleur-de-lis. Was he bringing Vicky lunch complete with poison? But she'd already been poisoned, so he couldn't be bringing it. Still, Gus was reluctant to cross him off the suspect list. In her experience, the spouse was often the killer.

As Gus moved away from the crime scene, her cop

instincts kicked in. Three reasons compelled her to solve the case. First, she couldn't resist the challenge, and maybe she was a little bored with nothing to do but play piano. Secondly, she was sworn to see justice served, and if there was a chance Winters would rule this as death by natural causes, then it would be up to Gus to find the killer. And thirdly—and possibly most importantly—Gus wanted to prove to Detective Winters that she was a good cop, perhaps even better than Winters herself.

CHAPTER 2

*R*uffled Feathers was on the street Gus had just come from, so she stuffed her sheet music in her pocket and headed back. The shop was in a brick building and had cheery feather garlands around the front door.

Taking care not to stand directly under one of the dagger-like icicles that hung from the roof's peak, she opened the door and entered.

The shop was filled with anything and everything to do with birds. Bird cages, bird feeders, bird food. If it had to do with birds, it was in there. One wall was loaded with cuckoo clocks, some of which were adorned with carved birds while others had birds waiting to pop out of the doors when the hour chimed.

Behind the counter stood two women, one of whom

was the blonde who had spoken from the edge of the crowd. The other was an almost identical copy of her.

They looked up as Gus approached. "Can we help you?" they said in unison then looked at each other and giggled.

Gus smiled. Normally, she'd start peppering them with questions, but she wasn't here in an official police capacity, so she supposed she'd have to act like a nosy busybody. That was what her sister Willa did to wheedle information out of people when she butted into her cases back home.

"Did you hear? That lady that spouts off about the birds just dropped dead out there." Gus acted nonchalant, looking through one of the displays of bird-themed greeting cards. She wasn't exactly sure that the girl who had been in the crowd knew that Vicky had died. She might have left before the woman collapsed. Either way, Gus was keen to see their reaction.

"Vicky Smithers?" one of them asked. Gus noticed they were wearing name tags. Apparently, one was named Comfort and the other Joy. Odd names, but she supposed if you lived in Christmas Village and gave birth to twins, they were appropriate.

Gus shrugged. "I think someone called her Vicky."

"Wait, she's dead?" Comfort looked at Joy. "I thought you said she passed out."

"I thought she did." Joy looked mildly disturbed. Was she just acting? Had she known that Vicky was dead? Maybe she'd left the scene early on purpose so as to not look too interested in the victim's fate.

"Afraid not. They weren't able to revive her." Not that anyone really tried to revive her, since it was clear that she was gone right away. Gus tried to look as if something had just dawned on her. "Oh, I suppose that's good news for you guys. Aren't you in charge of all the birds here in Christmas Village?"

"Yes, we are," Joy said cheerfully. "I mean, it's not good news for us, though. We didn't want anyone to die."

"How did she die?" Comfort asked.

Gus studied her to see if she was being coy. If Comfort and Joy had murdered Vicky, then they would know exactly how she died. "I don't know. She just keeled over."

"Heart attack?" Joy sounded like she was hoping the police would think that.

"She was kind of young for a heart attack, wasn't she?" Gus asked, trying to draw more information out of them.

"Yeah, but she got worked up about a lot of stuff," Comfort said. "Maybe all that stress and negativity did her in. What did the police say?"

"They mentioned something about natural causes."

Comfort and Joy stared at her. Did they appear to be relieved? If they'd poisoned Vicky, then they should be practically gleeful if the police would attribute the death to natural causes.

But there was a problem though. Comfort and Joy obviously weren't exactly on friendly terms with Vicky, so how would they have been able to get her to ingest poison? Comfort had been in the crowd. Could she have slipped Vicky something?

Gus made a mental note to see if she could find out when and what Vicky had last eaten and what poisons might be slower acting. Gus didn't remember any water or coffee cup around, so she didn't think someone had slipped it into anything Vicky was drinking. And if the husband was bringing her food, then that probably meant she hadn't just eaten, unless someone had given her a snack of some sort. Maybe a cookie or some chocolates or even fruitcake.

If she were assigned to this case as sheriff, she could simply find out what the victim had eaten from the autopsy. She could probably find out what type of poison had killed her, too, if it was indeed poison. But she wasn't working this case in an official capacity. She'd have to resort to sneakier methods.

For the first time, she realized how hard it must be

for Willa to investigate all those murders back home. Maybe she should go easier on her. Willa did come up with some halfway decent solutions, and Gus grudgingly admitted her efforts did help solve the crime, *sometimes*. Gus had never realized before how difficult that must be even with Willa's unnaturally smart cat.

She inspected one of the large bird cages. "I suppose it is disturbing when someone in the village dies, but without her around, your lives will be a lot easier, right?"

"Sure!" Joy eagerly agreed. "She was making quite a ruckus, and people were starting to... hey...wait a minute, you're not insinuating that we killed her, are you?"

"No, of course not. Though I did hear something about her getting your bird-keeping permits pulled..."

Comfort and Joy started fluttering behind the counter. "Not true. Well, she did try, but we've done nothing wrong."

"Yeah, we keep the birds happy and healthy. Just look at them." Joy gestured toward the window that overlooked the village green. High atop bountiful nests in a shed decorated like a Swiss chalet sat the geese-a-laying. All six of them seemed to be happily settled into their cozy nests. At the far end of the pond, the swans a-swimming glided blissfully. Beyond the swans was a tree laden with golden delicious pears. A little brown bird—the partridge, Gus presumed—poked its head out from under a shrub, looked around, and then darted back into the shrub. The partridge seemed happy. And Gus had heard the calling birds squawking their heads off earlier that morning. They were quite healthy, if the volume of their ear-piercing calls was any indication.

But just because the birds were healthy and happy didn't mean that Comfort and Joy hadn't killed Vicky.

"I suppose they do look happy, but still when people start poking around in your business, it can get sticky," Gus said.

Comfort and Joy glared at her. The vibe was no longer friendly, and Gus figured she might have worn out her welcome.

"Sure, it was a pain the way she kept putting up those flyers and spouting off about the birds, but our permits were in good standing, and we have no violations. Just ask Mary Dunn down at the town hall. She's in charge of making sure the tourist attractions are in compliance. She'll tell you we had nothing to worry about."

CHAPTER 3

*O*n the way home from Ruffled Feathers, Gus made a detour to the town offices to talk to Mary Dunn. The conversation would cut into her practice time, but suddenly solving this crime seemed much more important.

As she walked, she did an online search for poisons on her phone. There were a few that could be disguised in food and wouldn't take effect for an hour or so later. Was it possible someone had put something in Vicky's food earlier that morning? The husband might have shown up with the bag as a way to prove that he didn't give her food earlier, because if he had, why bring takeout now?

The town offices were just down the street from the

toy factory where Gus had heard they employed elves to make the toys. Seriously? She figured it was just a rumor the town perpetuated to keep up the persona of Christmas Village, which seemed to have all the usual tropes from childhood Christmas shows.

She passed the giant crossed candy canes in front of the toy factory door and turned down a cobblestone street lined with old buildings and classical architecture. The town offices were in an older brick building that had granite steps and carved concrete columns in front. Next to the steps, a snowman stood beside a Christmas tree that was decked out in blue and silver vintage style ornaments.

The doors opened into a marble-floored lobby. Luckily, signs were posted along the wall, and she found Mary Dunn's office quite easily. Gus tapped on the door.

"Come in!"

Mary's office wasn't anything like the stark governmental office she'd expected. The room was light and airy with white painted furniture, large windows, and lots of plants. Mistletoe, to be exact.

A middle-aged brunette sat behind the desk tying sprigs of mistletoe. Gus glanced up. She didn't want to get caught underneath the plant and have someone run in and kiss her unexpectedly. She hated surprises, especially if they involved kissing.

"Can I help you?"

"Umm, yes…" On the way down the hall, Gus had decided that she'd pretend to be doing research on the village for a news article. Town officials always liked to have their names in the paper, and since Mary was in charge of village tourism, she'd be eager to talk. "I was doing some research on Christmas Village for an article and people said you were the one to talk to."

Mary brightened and gestured to the chair across from her desk. "Please have a seat."

Gus picked up a sprig of mistletoe that had been lying on the seat of the chair, and Mary said, "Sorry, I'm making up some decorations to put about in the shops. We always like to put it out fresh near the holiday. You can just put that on the desk."

Gus put the sprig on the desk and sat in the chair. Hadn't she seen mistletoe listed as a poisonous plant when she did her Google search earlier? The birds were a big tourist attraction in Christmas Village, and if Vicky was complaining about their care, Mary probably wouldn't be too happy about that. If Vicky had been poisoned with Mistletoe, that would place Mary on Gus's suspect list. But how could she find out what substance was used to poison Vicky? Winters certainly wouldn't tell her. She needed to make friends with some of the locals and get tapped into the rumor mill.

Mary finished the red satin bow she'd been tying around the sprig with a flourish and turned to Gus, focusing on her. "Now, what can I tell you about the village?"

Gus took a deep breath and tried to phrase her questions the way someone writing an article would phrase them as opposed to the usual blunt line of questioning she used as a sheriff. "Well, Christmas Village is so different from other places. You've got the pipers piping, the maids a-milking, all the snowmen and decorations and birds. There must be criteria for all these things, I imagine, right?"

"Yes, of course. We have certain standards and pride ourselves in a realistic and unforgettable experience."

"And I suppose all of those attractions require permits of some sort?"

Mary frowned, looking suspicious of Gus's line of questioning. "Of course. We make sure everything is in order and has the proper permits as mandated by state law."

Gus plastered on a friendly smile and nodded enthusiastically to banish any fears Mary might have that she was some sort of undercover state inspector on a surprise visit. "Right, of course. I wanted to emphasize in the article how everything is safe and how well treated the animals are."

This last bit seemed to mollify Mary. "That's good. I appreciate that."

"What about the care of the cows that the maids milk, the horses that pull the sleighs, and the birds? I heard that lady outside saying that the birds aren't well cared for and should be removed from the village."

Mary made a dismissive noise. "Vicky Smithers. She's been spouting off about that for months now. All of our animals are well cared for, and the permits to house them here are in order. We have routine state inspections and have never failed one."

"So, those girls that take care of the birds weren't in any danger of losing their permits because of Vicky, then?"

Mary looked taken aback. "No. Well, I guess she was creating a bit of a ruckus, but I don't think it was going to amount to anything."

"I guess they won't have to worry about that anymore, anyway." Gus kept her voice casual and studied Mary for her reaction.

"What do you mean?" Mary looked her straight in the eye, but Gus couldn't tell if Mary already knew about the death. Surely, since she worked in the town hall, news would have spread to her already. Maybe she'd been too busy with the mistletoe. Or maybe she was only acting like she hadn't heard because she knew more about it than she should.

"The woman died not long ago."

Mary gasped. Her hand flew to her chest. "Really? I had no idea. What happened?"

"She was putting up one of those flyers and just dropped dead."

Mary frowned. "Dropped dead? You mean a heart attack? Come to think of it, she did get very worked up. Her face would turn all red. I bet she had a heart condition."

Before Gus could tell Mary that Vicky might not have died from natural causes, the door opened, and a woman in her early twenties peeked in. "Oh sorry, didn't know you had someone in here, Auntie."

Mary gestured for her to come in. "It's okay, dear. This is my niece Belinda. She's one of the maids a-milking."

"Nice to meet you," Gus said. "Speaking of which, I suppose there are all kinds of regulations about the milk used in the village too." Gus was trying to keep in character and not tip Mary off that she was only interested in the birds.

"Of course there is, but we followed them all,"

Belinda said eagerly. "That's why Auntie has to take me to the Good Tidings Café with my pail of milk. The milk has to be delivered within ten minutes, and it takes too long for me to walk all the way."

Mary grimaced. "Belinda was in a little bit of trouble last year and lost her driver's license. So I drive her for her deliveries."

"That's nice that you can do that. This is great info for my article." Gus stood. "I won't take up any more of your time."

At the door, Gus turned, remembering the note in Vicky's appointment book. Mary probably knew a lot of people in town and might be able to make sense of it.

"Before I go, I do have one more question. Is there someone in town with a name like Saint Nic who would have something to do with the birds or the permitting?"

Mary frowned. "Saint Nick? No, I don't think so. That's an odd name."

"It wasn't really *Saint* Nick. More like S-T N-I-C." Gus spelled out the letters she'd seen on the calendar. "An abbreviation, maybe?"

"Oh, I know!" Belinda said. "That must be Steven Nicholson. He's a lawyer in town. I have to meet with him for my probation. That's how I know. He looks over all the legal documents, including permits."

"Why do you ask that?" Mary asked.

"Just something I saw on a note." Lawyer? Interesting. Gus said goodbye and headed out. If Vicky had an appointment with a lawyer, that might mean she was about to take legal action. And *that* would mean the killer had an even more urgent motive.

CHAPTER 4

*G*us spent the rest of the afternoon familiarizing herself with the songs she and the sax player, Ivy Peterson, had agreed upon. She arrived at the North Pole Lounge precisely on time to meet her and practice a little before the customers started piling in.

A red sleigh with six reindeer attached was parked out front. The reindeer stamped their hooves and nodded their fuzzy antlers in her direction as she passed. Gus gave them a wide berth. She'd made the mistake of trying to pet one of the majestic creatures on her first day in town, and that had resulted in the whole team of reindeer making fun of her and calling her a Barbie doll. So what if she had long blonde hair, blue eyes, and an hourglass figure on the outside? On the inside she was tough, a competent officer of the law, and she was *certainly* no doll. And since when did reindeer talk anyway? Apparently that was part of the Christmas Village magic.

The North Pole Lounge had all the ambiance of a big-city jazz club. The club was dimly lit with candles on the black tables and twinkling miniature white lights in strategic places. The charcoal rug, dark gray walls, and black ceiling added to the chic-but-cozy ambiance.

The lounge had a long bar that ran the length of the wall opposite the door and was lit with a soothing blue light from underneath. The hour was early, and only two people sat at the bar. One of them was a large beefy man. It wasn't surprising to see someone like that here. What was surprising was the person he was talking to: Detective Winters.

Winters had a long paper in her hand, so long that it curled down onto the top of the bar like an old scroll. She was writing something at the top of it.

"Excuse me, are you Gus Chance?"

Gus turned to see a woman of about twenty-five. She was fresh faced with a smattering of freckles across her nose and an eager look in her periwinkle-blue eyes. The young woman was carrying a saxophone case, so it didn't take much detective work to figure out who it was. "Ivy Peterson?"

The girl nodded enthusiastically, her halo of strawberry blonde curls bobbing around her head. Her eyes drifted over to the bar, widening when she recognized Detective Winters. "Did you hear about what happened today?" she said in a low voice.

"The death? Yeah."

"They said natural causes but…"

Ivy let her voice trail off, and Gus cast her an appraising look. From the sound of it, the girl didn't believe it was natural causes, either, and the way she was staring at Detective Winters led Gus to believe she had an interest in the case.

"You don't think it was natural causes?" Gus said.

"Not really. I mean, she wasn't that old, and she *was* causing trouble in town. Some people might have wanted to get rid of her."

"My thoughts exactly," Gus said.

They both strained to overhear the conversation going on between Winters and the man at the bar, which was not very difficult because Winters was talking pretty loudly. Gus caught the words "…poisoned with hemlock."

Hemlock! Gus was mildly disappointed it wasn't

mistletoe, but then that would have been too easy since she knew exactly where to go to find that.

"Poisoned!" Ivy gasped.

Winters's gaze flicked in their direction. Her expression screwed up into a scowl when she recognized Gus. She pushed up from her stool, rolled up her scroll, and headed over to them.

"What are you doing here? Investigating?" Winters demanded. Gus resisted the urge to step back and apologize. She was on equal footing with Winters now and no longer the student.

"No. Playing jazz." Gus pointed at the shiny black baby grand piano in the corner. Ivy lifted her sax case.

Winters's scowl deepened. "You play jazz?"

"Yep."

Winters stared at her for a few minutes and then nodded. Her gaze drifted to Ivy and then back to Gus.

"Make sure you keep it to just playing jazz, Sherlock." Winters spun on her heel and left.

"That was weird," Ivy said. "Guess I was right about Vicky. Sounds like she was poisoned, which means she was murdered."

Gus wasn't sure what to make of Ivy. She was a little too excited about murder. "Sounds that way. You seem to be overly interested in Vicky's death. Why is that?"

"You don't think I always want to be a piper piping, do you? A girl's got to have ambitions, and mine is to be a police detective." Ivy looked sideways at Gus. "You seem overly interested, too, and why did Winters call you Sherlock?"

"I'm in law enforcement."

Piper looked at her admiringly. "Are you here investigating undercover?"

"Hardly. I'm here on vacation and to play jazz."

"Then why did it seem like Winters was warning you off? Sounds like you know her."

Gus sighed. She had to hand it to the girl—she was persistent if nothing else.

"She was my teacher at the police academy."

"So you're a detective too?"

"Sheriff."

Gus could practically see stars in the young saxophone player's eyes. "Are you sure you're not investigating? Because Winters seems to think so."

"I might have been a bit over-inquisitive at the crime scene. I thought Winters might be trying to get out of investigating by saying the death was natural, and I couldn't let that happen. But now it looks like she might be digging into it."

"So you *are* interested in investigating. I'd love to help."

Gus studied Ivy. She was enthusiastic and probably had good instincts if she'd figured that Vicky didn't die of natural causes. And she did know people in town, which would make getting information easier. Perhaps she could come in handy. "Maybe I could use some help. Do you know that guy at the bar that Winters was talking to?"

"Yule Navidad? Sure, he runs the reindeer transport and just took over the toy factory. Nice guy."

"Reindeer transport? Why do you think Winters was talking to him? She mentioned the poison to him, so they must have been talking about the case. Do you have any idea why he would be involved?"

"Do you think he's a suspect? As far as I know, he didn't know Vicky, and her complaints didn't really affect him because reindeer are supposed to live in this climate." Ivy pressed her lips together. "But nothing gets in or out of Christmas Village unless it comes in one of his sleighs. Maybe Winters was following a lead about a delivery for Vicky. Come on, I'll introduce you."

Gus followed Ivy to the bar, and they did a round of introductions. Yule looked Gus over. "You new in town, huh?"

"Just on vacation," Gus said. The last thing she

wanted was to encourage romance from some toy-producing sleigh driver.

Ivy got straight to the point. "We saw Winters here. Was she asking something about the murder?"

Yule smiled at her. "I figured you'd be around to ask." He turned to Gus. "Ivy here is a budding detective. She's a good kid, see?"

Gus nodded. "Yes, I see."

Then he turned back to Ivy. "She was asking about hemlock. Seems that lady was poisoned with hemlock. But not just any kind. It was fresh."

"Why would she be asking you about that?" Gus asked. She was skeptical about Winters's methods. Normally, police didn't spill their guts about these details to the citizens unless they were trying to trip up a suspect.

"Nothing gets in or out of Christmas Village without me knowing because I have the only shipping transport," Yule said. "Fresh produce or livestock requires special permits, and Winters wanted to know who got fresh produce in this week."

Yule sipped his cocktail, which was what Gus normally referred to as a frou-frou drink—a foamy blue concoction in a tall glass with lots of fruit around the rim. Not the sort of drink that she would expect a large man who looked like a mobster to drink, but she was learning that unusual things often happened in Christmas Village.

"So who got fresh produce?" Gus prompted after a few seconds when Yule didn't supply the information.

"No one. The only live thing that came in was a Pomeranian for Gladys, one of the elves at the toy factory." Yule's expression turned sad. "Her little Bitsy died last month, so we all pitched in and got her another puppy. She was happy."

"So no fresh plants came? Then someone must have grown it here," Gus said.

"It's not that easy," Ivy said. "The ground is frozen, and the days are short. You'd need special equipment to grow indoors."

"Winters asked about that too. No one ordered any grow lights or anything. I suppose they could have already had them, though." Yule turned to Gus. "So are you helping Ivy investigate this?"

Gus glanced at Ivy. "I guess you could say that."

Yule leaned closer to her. "Maybe I could help you out, see?"

Gus didn't see. And she didn't want Yule to help. Having to team up with Ivy would be bad enough. She usually worked alone, except when she had to call in help from the sheriff in the next county. She preferred to be on her own. Ivy seemed like a nice kid, but she was a necessity, someone who would have an "in" with the locals. Yule, on the other hand, would just get in the way.

Gus gave him a short smile. Nothing too encouraging. "We'll let you know if we need your help. Right now, I think we better try a practice set before the place fills up."

CHAPTER 5

*T*he next day Gus woke up to a cacophony of squawking. When she'd rented the apartment from Airbnb, they'd failed to mention that the calling birds were directly across the street. They made an awful racket every single morning. Luckily, there were only four of them.

The gig at the North Pole Lounge the night before had gone very well, although she could've done without Yule's extra attention. She was afraid he might be developing a bit of a crush on her, and she wanted to nip that in the bud while still keeping him as a future source. As it turned out, Ivy was an excellent saxophone player, and they had a lot of fun playing some of Gus's favorite jazz tunes. The customers had liked it, too, if the enthusiasm of their applause was any indication.

The evening of piano playing had invigorated her and the prospect of continuing her investigation this morning even more so. But even though Ivy was a good sax player and she was glad they'd teamed up at the lounge, Gus didn't relish the idea of having a sidekick in the investigation. The locals were her only source of information, though, and having Ivy around would help her talk to them without raising their suspicions too much. In her experience, people clammed up around strangers. Additionally, it would be a lot better to have someone whose investigation she could control, as opposed to her sister Willa, who was always running off doing things on her own that could potentially mess matters up for Gus.

Ivy arrived promptly at nine o'clock, as they'd arranged the night before, and they started going over the clues.

Gus's place was small, so they decided to walk around town, keeping their voices low so no one could overhear. Gus took care not to walk under the dangerous icicles dangling from the gutters and to keep out of earshot of the snowmen. She knew the snowmen were not real, but it still seemed like they were trying to listen in.

A light dusting of snow fell as it usually did, even though the sun was shining brightly. Skaters in colorful fur-lined outfits twirled on the pond, and the bells above the shop doors jangled as shoppers went in and out.

Horse-drawn sleighs clip-clopped down the street pulling tourists with hot cocoa mugs in their hands and blankets wrapped around their legs. Gus wasn't interested in any of the local scenery or attractions this morning, though. She wanted to get the bottom of this murder and prove to Winters that she wasn't the same flunky who'd screwed up back in the police academy.

"So far, we know the killer used fresh hemlock that had to be grown somewhere in the village. Do you have any idea who could do that?" Gus asked Ivy.

Ivy gestured toward the snow-covered ground. "Clearly no one can grow it in their gardens. Had to be indoors."

Gus pressed her lips together. "Well, unfortunately, that doesn't narrow it down too much, does it? Anyone could set up an indoor grow area with some grow lights, dirt, and fertilizer. I hope Winters has a search warrant out for her suspects so she can see if any of them have a grow room."

Ivy nodded. "I'm sure she does. We don't have that benefit, so we have to be sneakier."

"True. Let's work on some of the other things we know. We know Vicky had seen a lawyer, but we don't know why. Let's assume it had something to do with her pet project of shipping the Christmas Village birds south. Those girls that run Ruffled Feathers—Comfort and Joy—must have felt threatened by Vicky. She could have ruined their business, especially if she brought some kind of lawsuit."

"Pretty much everyone in the village would suffer if that happened. One of the big tourist draws is all the birds." Ivy gestured toward the lake, where they could see the swans a-swimming. This part of the lake was far from the skaters. Gus supposed they must have kept the water from freezing with aerators that keep it in motion.

"The swans are pretty, but I could do without those calling birds," Gus said grumpily.

Ivy laughed. "You got suckered into one of those Airbnbs across the street from them? They can be a little loud. Just be glad you're not near the drummers drumming. That incessant beat all night long is like dripping water torture."

They were at the very edge of the park now. A majestic pear tree towered over them, golden pears dripping off its lush green branches. The branches were so full of heavy pears that they drooped down almost to the grassy ground below. The tree was surrounded by shrubs and smaller trees that went quite a way toward the pond, like a secret forest. The bright green leaves were a striking contrast to the white snow in the background. A golden fence roped off the area.

Gus stopped in her tracks. "Wait a minute. This pear tree and all the shrubs are thriving in the middle of winter."

"Of course. They sell the pears at the market. And of course, the partridge in the pear tree is a big tourist attraction, especially since its pears are in season all year long."

A bird about the size of a chicken poked its head out. It had pretty brown feathers on the wings and gray on its chest. Its face was white with black markings on the sides and neck. Black, beady eyes sized them up.

"*Squawk!*"

"He doesn't sound very welcoming," Gus said.

"Yeah, the town frowns against anyone going near him or the pear tree. That's why the fence is here."

"Well, what makes the tree and shrubs grow in winter?" Gus asked as the partridge craned its neck out farther while still keeping to the safety of the shrub it had been squatting under. Something was odd about the bird. His feathers looked puffy and over-preened.

"No one knows. There's a lot of things about Christmas Village that are… well… sort of magical."

"If a pear tree and shrubs can grow in there, maybe hemlock can." Gus swung one leg over the fence. "We need to check it out."

"Hey! You can't go in there!" Comfort appeared, practically out of nowhere, and yanked Gus off the fence.

"Hey, let go of me." Gus shook her arm free.

Comfort dropped Gus's arm then stood with her hands fisted on her hips. "You can't go in there. That's the partridge in the pear tree."

Gus glanced over at the partridge. The bird had retreated under the shrub, and only a few tail feathers stuck out. "Technically, he's not *in* the pear tree. He's under that shrub."

"Yeah, so? Partridges don't sit in trees. Guess they didn't know that when they made up the song. The tourists don't seem to mind, though. They just like to see a partridge and a pear tree." Comfort gestured in the direction of the partridge and then the tree. She sounded very defensive. She kept darting glances at the shrubs, which only made Gus more determined to get inside. "It's a very important display in the village, and we don't want it ruined."

"Yeah, I see that. I wasn't going to hurt the partridge or the pear tree. I was looking at the other plants. I wanted to see what was growing in here."

"There's nothing growing there. It's just a pear tree and some shrubs. That's what it does—it grows." Comfort said. She still seemed very upset, her face red and voice shaky. She really was overprotective of her birds, or perhaps there was some other reason she didn't want Gus to go in there. "We don't need anyone messing with our partridge. It's bad enough that people throw rocks at the calling birds."

"Can't blame them, especially when those things go off so early in the morning," Gus muttered.

Comfort frowned at her. "Wait. You were the one asking questions in our store the other day, weren't you?"

"Yeah." Okay, so the girl was a little slow on the uptake. That didn't necessarily mean she lacked what it took to poison Vicky, or did it?

"We don't need anyone nosing around here. We have enough trouble." Comfort glanced at Ivy as if Ivy had committed treason by hanging around with Gus. "Don't we, Ivy?"

"If you mean the recent murder, I suppose we do," Ivy said.

The partridge let out a loud squawk, and Comfort jerked her head in that direction. "See? Now you've upset the partridge." She shooed them away from the

43

fence. "Go. Be on your way or I'll call Detective Winters."

Ivy raised a brow at Gus, and Gus nodded toward the road. Neither one of them wanted Detective Winters to come and yell at them.

"That was kind of weird behavior, don't you think?" Gus asked when they were out of earshot.

Ivy looked back over her shoulder. "Yeah, but Comfort and Joy are a little weird to begin with. They're very protective of the birds."

"Or maybe she was being protective of something else. What if she's the killer? She has a motive and could grow fresh hemlock right under the pear tree," Gus said.

"She could, but how would she get Vicky to eat it? They weren't exactly friends, so I doubt they could just bake her some brownies and expect her to chow down."

Gus paused to let a horse-drawn sleigh pass before crossing the street. "Good question. Maybe they got it to her through someone else or somehow snuck it into her food. According to my research, she could have eaten anywhere up to an hour before. Funny thing, though: her husband was bringing her a takeout bag, which would seem to indicate she hadn't eaten."

Ivy frowned. "A takeout bag? From where?"

Gus shrugged. "I didn't see any name on it. It was white with a blue fleur-de-lis."

Ivy nodded and thought for a few seconds. "Didn't you say you thought Vicky had an appointment with Steven Nicholson?"

"Yep. That's why I figure someone had to kill her right away. She might have been looking into some kind of lawsuit about the birds."

"Either that, or maybe she found out about the affair."

Gus jerked her gaze to Ivy. "Affair?"

"Yes, well, I didn't say anything before because it's just a rumor, but I have heard Vicky's husband Kevin was having an affair with Wanda Garland. She owns the Good Tidings Café. What if Vicky was seeing Nicholson because she was getting a divorce?"

"Would her husband not want a divorce? Seems like if he was having an affair, that would be welcome unless Vicky had money that he would stand to lose in a divorce."

Ivy shrugged. "Exactly. I don't know their financial situation, but there's something else that might point to the husband."

"What's that?"

"The Good Tidings Café has takeout bags that are white with a blue fleur-de-lis on them."

Gus thought about that for a minute. "But the husband came onto the scene after Vicky was dead. He was bringing the takeout bag after she was poisoned." Wasn't he?

Ivy looked at Gus. "Maybe that's what he wanted everyone to think. Did you see him arrive with the bag? Can you be sure the bag wasn't already on the scene? What if he cleverly planned it so that he could swoop in and grab the bag, making it look like he'd just arrived with it and thus taking away the only evidence of how Vicky ingested the poison."

Gus stared at Ivy. She couldn't remember seeing the bag before. Nor did she recall whether the husband had arrived with it or picked it up at the scene. He'd made a big fuss over the body. Had the bag been there near her things? Gus couldn't remember, but the theory was worth investigating.

CHAPTER 6

The Good Tidings Café was an old-fashioned diner at the north end of Main Street. Outside, a sign boasted that they used fresh-grown herbs. Yet another thing to make the owner suspicious: if she grew herbs for cooking, then she'd be able to grow hemlock.

The inside gleamed with chrome. Naugahyde booths and metal-edged Formica tables sat under a row of large windows that looked out over the scenic village. Across from the door was a long counter with round stools. The top of the counter was punctuated with glass cake stands, each filled with some kind of pastry.

"That's her," Ivy whispered, nodding toward a tall brunette who was taking an order at one of the booths.

Gus supposed the woman was pretty in a practical sort of way. She looked to be in her early forties, the same age as the victim, so she would be a likely candidate for an affair with the husband.

They took seats at the counter, and Gus resisted the urge to spin around on the stool as she used to do when she was a kid. Across from the counter, a pass-through looked into the kitchen, where a thin woman slaved over a flat top. The smell of bacon and sausage wafted out. Gus's stomach growled. She hadn't had breakfast yet.

"Order up!" Wanda shouted as she slipped behind the counter and clipped the order slip onto a spinning rack on the pass-through. She turned to Ivy and Gus.

"Hi, Ivy." Wanda nodded at Gus and then poised her pencil over the order pad. "What can I get you?"

She didn't look like an adulterer—or a murderer, for that matter. If the husband had killed Vicky, it didn't necessarily follow that Wanda would've known about it. Then again, Gus had seen plenty of killers who didn't look or act like killers.

"I'll have two eggs over medium, sausage, and toast," Gus said.

"I'll have the oatmeal." Ivy patted her stomach. "Watching my weight."

Gus looked down at her own stomach. It was flat as ever.

"So, quite a bit of excitement yesterday morning," Ivy said to Wanda.

Gus admired how Ivy just jumped right in with the questioning while acting as if she were simply gossiping. This stealth investigating was a challenge, and Gus would be happy if she never had to do it again. She had a new appreciation for how difficult it must be for her sister to butt into her investigations back home, which made why she always seemed to do it all the more curious. Then again, she always had been nosy, even as a little kid.

Wanda whipped out a cleaning cloth and started wiping down the counter. "I'll say. The café has been abuzz with it."

"Yeah, we heard the victim's a regular here," Gus said casually.

Wanda blinked. Her eye twitched. She scrubbed at the counter harder. "She did eat here, yeah."

"No wonder. The food must be great with all those fresh herbs and everything," Gus said.

Wanda glanced up at Gus. "The fresh herbs are a big draw."

"So what dishes do you put the herbs in?" Gus craned her neck to see into the kitchen, expecting to find pots full of herbs, but all she saw were eggs and sausages on the griddle. Her mouth watered. She hoped those were for her.

"Oh, the usual things, soups, sandwiches. Our omelet and breakfast sandwich specials."

"I heard the woman who died might have eaten her last meal here. Her husband picked it up for her." Gus lifted her brow as if to indicate that was suspicious.

"Her husband? I don't think so. Vicky usually came in by herself. In fact, she was here yesterday morning by herself." Wanda's voice was a bit high pitched, and the way her gaze darted around the café told Gus she was uncomfortable with this line of questioning. Perhaps she did have something to hide. But if Wanda was the killer, would she so readily admit that Vicky had gotten a breakfast sandwich from this café right before her death?

"She was?"

"Yeah. She always gets the breakfast sandwich special." Wanda pointed to the menu above the pass-through, where the breakfast sandwich complete with fresh herbs was listed. Ivy frowned up at the menu, and Gus knew what she was thinking. Wanda was practically confessing to being the killer by admitting Vicky had gotten her last meal there and then pointing out the breakfast sandwich had fresh herbs. Surely it would be easy enough to slip some hemlock in there unnoticed.

"So, you saw her get the sandwich?" Ivy asked.

Wanda nodded. "I took her order. I mean, I assume she got the sandwich. It gets busy in the mornings, and the other waitress must have rung her up. I was putting the milk into glass containers. I don't know why they bring it in a bucket. It's ridiculous."

"Yeah, that does seem crazy. I guess it's part of the village charm?" Gus asked, glancing at Ivy.

Ivy nodded. "The maids a-milking are an attraction, and the restaurants all use our own fresh milk. The town thinks it's quaint for people to see the maids bring it around in a bucket. It's all sterilized, though, so don't worry."

At least Wanda wasn't lying about the milk. Belinda had said she came every morning with her bucket.

Wanda started edging away from them, and Gus went in for the kill with the most important question. "So where do you get fresh herbs around here? Do you grow them?"

"Yep. Grown right on the premises in a special room off the kitchen."

"Order up!" The cook placed a plate and a bowl on the pass-through.

Wanda looked relieved to have a reason to turn away. She slid the dishes in front of Ivy and Gus.

"You ladies enjoy." Wanda slipped out from behind the counter, grabbing the coffee pot on her way to top off the customers in the booths.

Gus looked at her plate carefully to make sure no unwanted herbs—like hemlock—had made their way on it. Then she broke into one of the eggs with her fork and watched the orange yolk ooze out onto the plate. She used the toast to sop up some yolk as she thought about Wanda's odd behavior. If she were the killer, why would she admit so readily to Vicky being here? But if she wasn't the killer, then why had she seemed like she was hiding something?

CHAPTER 7

*G*us hoped that Wanda wasn't the killer because the breakfast was delicious. She'd hate to see the diner close down, even though she was only staying in town for a few more days.

"That was a little confusing," Ivy said as they walked back along the street.

"Yeah, very confusing. On the one hand, she acted like she was hiding something, but on the other, she was practically pointing us toward the fact that Vicky had been there that morning." Gus glanced at Ivy out of the corner of her eye. "By the way, good technique getting her to open up."

Ivy blushed and shrugged it off. "I watch a lot of detective shows."

"Maybe Wanda was acting nervous because she's having the affair with Vicky's husband." Gus replayed the conversation in her mind. "Come to think of it, she did start to act funny once I mentioned him."

"She had no qualms about pointing out the fresh herbs were grown there on the premises, and you'd think if she'd grown hemlock to poison Vicky, she might want to keep that on the down-low."

Gus wrapped her olive-green scarf tighter around her neck. "She might not even know Vicky was poisoned. She might not be in on it. Could be just the husband."

"But the husband didn't touch the sandwich. Wanda said that Vicky was there alone," Ivy said.

"Which begs the question of why the husband had a bag when he showed up at the crime scene. He might not have brought it, like you suggested," Gus said. "He could have slipped the hemlock in after Vicky picked it up. And if he did that, then he'd want to make sure the bag didn't get collected by the police."

"And he'd be watching to see when she keeled over, then swoop in and grab the bag before anyone noticed." Ivy pressed her lips together. "But then he would have had to grow the hemlock. Unless he and Wanda were in on it together."

They'd been so engrossed in talking about the clues that they'd walked all the way to the pear tree without realizing it. The partridge was peering out from under a shrub, watching them intently. As Gus watched, a feather dropped off his wing. More feathers lay on the ground. Was the bird molting? Would that happen if a bird ate hemlock? And if hemlock was under there, who had planted it?

Maybe Kevin Smithers *had* acted alone. Just because Wanda had a room where she grew fresh herbs didn't prevent Kevin from growing hemlock in his own room or even under the pear tree.

"So what do we do next?" Ivy asked.

"If this was something I was investigating as the sheriff, I'd find out where the husband was shortly before Vicky's death and get a search warrant for the house. But since I'm not working in an official capacity, I can't ask him, and I doubt Winters is going to give us that information."

"Winters must have already asked him, but she hasn't arrested him. What does that tell us?" Ivy asked.

"One of two things. Either the husband has an alibi that proves he couldn't have slipped anything into the wife's food that morning, or she doesn't have enough proof to nail him on it," Gus said.

"We need to find something that ties the killer to the murder."

"We know the killer grew hemlock. We can't search people's homes, but we can easily find a way to look at the herb grow room at the café. If Wanda is involved, we might find hemlock there."

"And if we don't, it could rule her out, but we'd still have the husband as a suspect."

Gus glanced at the partridge. "And let's not forget Comfort and Joy. Comfort was very upset that I might climb that fence. I think we need to rule out our suspects one at a time, though."

"So, we need to get a look at that room off the kitchen over at Good Tidings," Ivy said. "But it's off the kitchen. I doubt Wanda is going to let us go waltzing into the kitchen."

"Maybe not as customers, but I think I know another way that we can get in there."

Mary seemed surprised when Gus and Ivy showed up at her office. The place was still loaded with mistletoe, and Gus couldn't help but scan the area for hemlock, but she didn't spot any of the feathery leaves or tiny white flowers that she'd seen when she searched

Google.

Mary smiled at Gus. "How is your article coming along?"

Ivy frowned at Gus, but Gus poked her in the ribs. She'd forgotten to tell Ivy about her cover story.

"Good. Actually, I'm following up on something for the article and have a favor to ask."

Mary's gaze turned suspicious. "Of me?"

"Yes, I wanted a behind-the-scenes look at the milk and how it's delivered, so we were hoping we could take Belinda on her milk run to the Good Tidings Café," Gus said.

Mary's gaze drifted from Gus to rest on Ivy. Her brow was creased in a slight frown, as if she wondered why Ivy was even there. Then her brows rose a few centimeters, and her mouth formed a little O.

"Wait a minute. I've heard you're some sort of amateur sleuth, Ivy." She looked back at Gus. "You aren't writing an article about the village, are you? You're writing about Vicky's death."

Oh-oh. Busted. Gus shifted on her feet waiting for Mary to throw them out. "You could say that."

Mary pushed up from her desk, but instead of being angry, she looked intrigued. "And you think there is a clue at Good Tidings?"

Her interest took Gus by surprise, but she went with it. "Yes. The fresh herbs."

"Aha!" Mary snapped her fingers and started to pace. "I knew there was something funny about Wanda, and I'd heard about her and Kevin. Of course it makes sense they would be the main suspects."

"She told us she grows herbs right there on the premises, and Vicky was poisoned with an herb. But the room is off of the kitchen, and we need an excuse to get into the kitchen so we can try to get in that room. We figured if we went in with Belinda, that could be our excuse."

Mary looked skeptical. "But isn't this something that Detective Winters should be doing?"

Gus's stomach clenched. She didn't want Mary to refuse to help her or to tell Winters what they were up to. She wanted to solve the case herself. "Yes, but I'm a sheriff back in Mystic Notch, and I'm just following up on some of these leads. Winters and I go way back." It wasn't totally a lie. She just hoped Mary would make the erroneous conclusion that she was following the leads at Winters's request.

Mary brightened. "Oh. Sure, take Belinda, then. She's expecting me to pick her up at two-fifty."

"Great. Thanks." Gus turned to leave.

"So the police think the husband and Wanda were in on it together?" Mary asked.

Gus shrugged. She really had no idea what the police thought. "Well, we can't say for sure, but it's something to check on."

"Indeed. Well, good luck!"

"For a minute there, I thought Mary was going to call the cops on us," Ivy said once they were back out on the street.

"I know. I didn't like to lie, but I had to say something to make it seem official."

"That was quick thinking, though I do wonder if Detective Winters is on the same path as us," Ivy said.

Gus shrugged. "If Winters is halfway as good as she used to be, she will be onto this. But maybe she has been working other angles and just hasn't arrived at this conclusion yet."

Ivy glanced at the watch on her wrist. "Okay so should we meet around two-thirty?"

"Sure. Wait…there's one problem. The milking barn is almost a half mile out of town. How are we going to pick her up?"

Ivy smiled. "I've got you covered. I happen to have wheels. I can pick you up and then we'll head to the milking barn."

Gus frowned. "Your wheels aren't propelled by reindeer or horses, are they?"

"Nope, an old AMC Pacer."

Gus supposed a decades-old car that looked like a bubble was better than a team of sarcastic reindeer. "Good, then see you at two-thirty."

CHAPTER 8

*G*us spent the rest of the day picking up some Christmas gifts. She didn't have a long list to buy for but still found a beautiful engraved silver bookmark for her sister Willa and even a catnip toy for Willa's cat, Pandora. She was eager to visit the café and felt certain that either Wanda or Kevin was the killer.

At two twenty-five, Gus grabbed her black down jacket and stood outside to wait for Ivy. Across the street, a snowman appeared to study her, his red scarf dangling, carrot nose twitching. It wasn't really moving, was it?

She was more than happy to leave its scrutinizing gaze when Ivy pulled up.

The maids a-milking were situated in a large barn

on the edge of Christmas Village. The barn was a tourist attraction where the maids sat on their milking stools and tourists filed inside to watch. At the end of the barn was a sampling room where they could sample the fresh raw milk.

Belinda was already waiting in the pickup area with her pail of milk. She seemed surprised to see Gus and Ivy.

"Mary was busy, so we offered to pick you up," Ivy said.

Belinda shrugged. "Okay. As long as I'm not late. Wanda expects this milk promptly on time."

"You won't be late. Hop in." Belinda hopped into the back of the car, and they drove the short distance to the Good Tidings Café.

Wanda was surprised and possibly a little irritated to see them at the back door to the kitchen. "What are you doing here?"

"We gave Belinda a ride." Ivy shoved Belinda and her pail of milk into the kitchen. Then she and Gus slipped in behind her.

Wanda took the pail from Belinda and put it on the counter. Her eyes were trained on Gus as Gus wandered around.

"Thanks. Well, that's it, then." Wanda opened the door and gestured for them to leave.

Gus pretended not to notice. "This is fascinating. Really clean kitchen."

"Thank you." Wanda smiled, but her eyes were flat and filled with weariness and caution.

"The food smells delicious. Those fresh herbs really make the food top-notch." Gus scanned the chopped-up food on a cutting board in the counter. She saw some green stuff that she assumed was herbs, but they were small flakes and looked dry. "You must have a big area back here to grow them in." Gus craned her neck as if looking around the room for the herb-growing area.

"It's just a room." Wanda took several glass milk bottles down from a cabinet then lifted the lid off the pail and started transferring the milk into the bottles. "Now if you don't mind, we're kind of busy." Wanda gestured toward the door again.

"Oh, we don't mind. I love to see how you cook food in a restaurant," Gus said. "I'm not very good at cooking myself."

Wanda sighed. "We really don't want anyone in the kitchen while we're cooking. Health board violations and all that."

"Of course." Gus saw one door other than the one they'd come in through and edged toward it. "This must be the room where the famous herbs are grown."

Wanda jerked her gaze toward the door, spilling milk all over the counter. "You can't go in there!"

"Why not?" Gus had put her hand on the knob.

Wanda rushed over and stood in front of the door in an overly dramatic way, which obviously meant she had something to hide. Gus was starting to feel like she'd have this case wrapped up by dinner time. "We have special grow lights on timers, and there's a delicate watering system. The herbs are very sensitive. Opening the door would be bad. Very, very bad."

Wanda was babbling now, which only solidified her guilt even more in Gus's mind.

"That sounds fascinating. I'll just take a quick peek." Gus pulled on the knob.

Wanda put her palm on the door. "No you won't."

Gus pulled harder. "What's the harm, unless there's something you don't want me to see in there?"

All activity in the kitchen had stopped. Even the cook had stopped chopping. Everyone was watching them.

Wanda gnawed on her bottom lip. Clearly, she was nervous. "No! It's just that the herbs are so important."

"Good then you'll want me to see them." Gus hip-checked her out of the way and whipped the door open.

Gus gasped. What she saw inside the room was not what she expected.

There were no herbs. There were no grow lights or hydroponic systems dripping with water. There was a desk. A small table and chairs. A television.

And Kevin Smithers sitting at the table eating a sandwich.

Ivy crowded into the doorway beside Gus. "Wait. Where are the herbs?" Ivy asked.

Wanda sighed. "Okay, fine. You caught me. There are no fresh herbs. Happy now?"

Gus wasn't happy. She was disappointed. The room didn't even have so much as a cactus plant. No dirt. No sign of hemlock. Just a guilty-looking widower with mustard on the corner of his lips staring at them over a pastrami sandwich.

Gus turned to Wanda. "You didn't want us to come in here because there are no herbs?"

Wanda fiddled with her apron. "Yes," she said in a small voice. "I tried growing herbs in here—I really did —but there's just not enough light, even with grow lights, and the temperature never gets warm enough. So I get dried ones." She gestured toward the bookshelf, where a row of large plastic containers full of dried herbs sat. Gus scanned the labels. Basil, oregano, lemon balm, but no hemlock, of course.

Then again, Kevin Smithers *was* hiding in there with a guilty look on his face.

Gus gestured between Wanda and Kevin. "But you two are obviously up to something. Otherwise why would he be hiding in here? And I bet that *something* has to do with Vicky's death."

Kevin dropped his sandwich. "I'm not hiding! Well, I guess I am sort of hiding. We just didn't want to take our relationship public so soon after Vicky's death."

"Why not?" Ivy asked. "Afraid it might look suspicious?"

Wanda rushed to Kevin's side. "No! We just thought it was disrespectful."

"Yeah." Kevin stood and put his arm around Wanda's waist. "We didn't have anything to do with her death!"

Gus's eyes narrowed. "Oh no? Then why did Kevin have a takeout bag from this restaurant at the scene of the crime?"

Wanda gasped. She turned to Kevin. "Takeout bag?"

"That's right," Gus said. "You lied to me about Vicky coming in and getting her breakfast that morning, didn't you?"

Wanda shook her head vigorously. "No! She was here that morning, just like always."

"And you didn't give a takeout bag to Kevin, maybe one with something special in it?" Gus asked.

"I have no idea what you're talking about." Wanda's gaze flicked from Gus to Kevin. "Kev, what is she talking about?"

Kevin swallowed hard. "I think I know. I *was* there when Vicky died, except I didn't know what was happening. I was on my way home after punching out at the tinsel factory, and I saw all the commotion. I never imagined it was because Vicky had collapsed!" He glanced up at Wanda. "I'm sorry, but I heard this lady here say something about her being poisoned. I saw the Good Tidings takeout bag, and well…I thought maybe…" Kevin's voice drifted off, and he looked at Wanda with guilt-ridden eyes.

Wanda stepped away from him. "You thought what?"

Ivy glanced at Gus and then back to Kevin. "You mean you picked up the bag because you thought Wanda was the one who poisoned her?"

Kevin nodded, his gaze down at the floor. "I was afraid there might be evidence on the bag, so I grabbed it."

"And what was in it?" Gus asked.

"Nothing. It was empty. Not even a crumb."

"What did you do with it?"

"I threw it away." Kevin turned pleading eyes to Wanda. "Please don't be mad at me. I know you're not a killer, but when I saw her dead, and there was talk of poison, and the bag was just lying there next to her purse, I figured I'd grab it just in case. I only wanted to protect you from suspicion."

Wanda looked undecided. But then her face softened. She hugged him and brushed the mustard off his lip. "I don't like that you thought I *might* have killed her, but you risked getting caught with the bag to protect me, and that's all that matters."

They kissed, and Gus made a face. "You two still seem pretty suspicious to me. And I heard Vicky was seeing a lawyer. Maybe you didn't want her to divorce you and give up all that money."

"Money? What money?" Kevin asked.

"She had money that you'd lose in a divorce." Gus was bluffing, but why else wouldn't he just divorce her?

"Umm, no. She doesn't have any money. I just couldn't bring myself to tell her. I knew about the lawyer, though. She wasn't seeing him about a divorce."

"Yeah, that would have been too convenient for us," Wanda muttered.

"What was she seeing him about?" Ivy asked.

Kevin shook his head. "It was about those birds. She had a real bee in her bonnet about that. She was going to take up some kind of action to make sure they got better treatment."

Normally Gus, would be able to verify this with the lawyer, but she couldn't do that in this case. She'd just have to hope that Winters had already figured this out and was doing the checking. Still, she could ask a few questions to find out more. "You said you came upon the crime scene after punching out of work. Were you there all morning?"

Kevin nodded. "I worked the early shift at the tinsel factory. My shift had just ended, and I was walking home when I saw the crowd."

"See?" Wanda said. "If he was at work all morning, then he couldn't be the killer. I mean, I assume someone would have had to have given the poison to Wanda that morning shortly before she died."

Gus's gaze swiveled to Wanda. "That's right. And she did get food from this café."

"That's preposterous! I certainly couldn't have killed her. I was busy with the morning rush at that time." Wanda gestured around the room. "And, as you can see, I don't have any fresh herbs, much less fresh hemlock."

"Yeah. I saw her. She was busy with customers." Belinda, who had been watching with evident interest, chimed in. "By the way, I have to get back to the milking barn if you guys are done here."

"We'll be done in a sec." Gus turned back to Wanda. "You could have gotten fresh hemlock from somewhere else." But where? "Either one of you could be growing them at home."

Wanda sighed. "If I could grow stuff at home, don't you think I'd grow the herbs for my café there? But, as you can see, I have to resort to dried herbs."

"Yeah. You can check our houses." Kevin frowned. "Wait a minute. Why are we telling *you* this? *You're* not the police. And you can't check our houses. What are you even doing here?"

"Just following up. I'm the sheriff in Mystic Notch, New Hampshire," Gus said, omitting the fact that she really wasn't on any official capacity here.

They both looked skeptical, and she figured she'd better make her exit. She'd gotten everything she could out of them, anyway. Disappointment bloomed—she didn't think either Wanda or Kevin was the killer, but if not, then where did that leave her?

CHAPTER 9

*a*fter dropping Belinda off, Ivy and Gus sat in Ivy's car outside the cider shop and watched the lights come on in the Christmas trees as twilight approached. Darkness fell early in Christmas Village, which added to the ambiance. The tiny twinkling lights glowed more brightly, and the warm yellow light spilling from the shop windows seemed cozier after dark. But Gus knew everything wasn't cozy—a killer still walked the streets.

"Do you think they were lying?" Ivy asked.

Gus watched her breath steam up the window. "I'm not sure. Why would they kill Vicky and not just have Kevin divorce her? If what Kevin said about her not having money is true, there would be no reason to kill her."

"What if he was lying?" Ivy asked

"Unfortunately, we don't have the resources to dig into their finances."

Ivy frowned. "They did seem sincere, though."

Gus snorted as she opened the car door. "I've seen killers lie sincerely before."

"I suppose. So now what? We just give up? Wait for Winters to do something to check out their stories and then act on what she finds?"

Gus assumed Winters would be checking this all out. She and Noel would be able to get the proper warrants. Gus didn't have time to wait around for that to happen, and besides, she didn't think Wanda and Kevin were the killers.

Gus shook her head. "I don't want to just give up, but I'm not sure what to do next."

"Maybe we should practice. We're playing at the North Pole Lounge again tonight, right?" Ivy asked.

"Good idea." Gus got out of the car, then leaned in the passenger side window to talk to Ivy. "Maybe if we take our minds off of the case by practicing our music, something will bubble up from our subconscious."

"Hello there! How did it go?"

Gus turned to see Mary Dunn standing next to her on the sidewalk. She was holding a large bag with wrapped presents sticking out of the top. "Thanks for taking Belinda to the café. I took the opportunity to do some shopping."

"You're welcome."

She came closer to Gus and whispered, "I haven't heard anything. Did you manage to find the poison?"

Ivy had gotten out of the car to join in the conversation, and she and Gus shook their heads. "No. In fact, the husband claims to have an alibi, and Wanda says she was busy with other customers and didn't even wait on Vicky, though she does admit Vicky was there."

Mary nodded, pressing her lips together. "Well, I assume they would say that. Wouldn't they?"

"I'm sure they've told Detective Winters the same story. I suspect she'll check up on all that." Gus shrugged. "Funny thing, though. Wanda was guilty of one thing."

Mary frowned. "You mean besides being 'the other woman'?"

Gus nodded. "She doesn't actually use fresh herbs at the café. Says it's too hard up here even with indoor grow lights and such."

Mary clucked and nodded sympathetically. "It sure is. A lot of people have tried to grow things. Seems like the only place conducive to that is the pear tree."

Gus's gaze drifted in the direction of the pear tree. She could just barely see it from here, but she remembered the earth underneath and the golden juicy pears, not to mention the way Comfort had yanked them out from under the tree as if to keep Gus and Ivy from discovering something.

"You know, you might be on to something there."

Mary gave her a quizzical look. "Really? What do you mean?"

"Oh nothing…" Gus had focused her attention on the tree.

Mary shrugged. "Okay, then, I'm going to continue with my shopping. I'm sure it will all get straightened out."

They watched Mary walk off, then Gus turned to Ivy. She was just about to suggest looking under the pear tree when Yule came clomping down the street in his sleigh. The reindeer snorted and tossed their heads as they pulled up beside the Pacer.

The lead reindeer looked down at the car and then at his fellow teammates and rolled his eyes. "Would you get a load of that? A bubble car."

"Hey, no making fun of my mode of transportation, you fancied-up moose," Ivy said.

"No teasing the reindeer!" Yule gave Ivy a disapproving look. "I'm glad I caught up with youse. Are you gonna be playing tonight?"

"Yes." Gus's eagerness to play at the lounge was dampened by the way Yule looked her up and down.

"Good. I'm gonna have a first-row seat at one of the tables, see?"

"Great." Gus forced a smile. Luckily, she was only staying here through the end of the week. She didn't know how long it would be before she'd have to resort to rudeness for Yule to get the message that she wasn't interested.

"Anyways, I remembered you girls were asking about any live shipments, and I wanted to tell you one came in today."

"For who?"

"Ruffled Feathers. It was a big box, and they hurried down to get it right quick, too, so I think it must have been important."

Once again, Gus's gaze drifted down toward the pear tree. Of course, a live shipment didn't mean much of anything now. Vicky had already been poisoned. But this knowledge just made it all that more evident that all the clues pointed toward Comfort and Joy.

Yule flicked the reins, and the reindeer started forward. "Well, see you girls tonight!"

As Yule trotted off, Ivy turned to Gus. "I think he likes you."

Gus rolled her eyes. "Not interested. But what I am interested in is the live shipment."

"Why? Vicky was already poisoned, so it couldn't be hemlock unless Comfort and Joy are planning on going on a poisoning spree."

"I'm not sure how the box figures in, but I am sure of one thing. Kevin said Vicky was seeing Stephen Nicholson about bringing some legal action about the birds. That would definitely affect Comfort and Joy, and they can clearly grow things over there near the pear tree."

Ivy pressed her lips together. "Comfort did seem overly upset when we were poking around there before."

"And that partridge was looking kind of ragged the last time I saw it. Maybe that's because it was eating hemlock. We already know that Comfort and Joy had a motive. If we can find hemlock in that area, then we can prove they had means. Then, hopefully, we can hit them with the evidence and get them to confess." Gus turned to Ivy. "Go drop off your car, dress in something dark, and meet me at the tree in thirty minutes."

CHAPTER 10

The sky was dark by the time Gus and Ivy met at the pear tree. The tree itself was subtly lit with a soft spotlight and a sparse smattering of twinkling lights that seemed to highlight each juicy pear. The area around the tree was cloaked in shadows. Ivy arrived dressed in a black shirt and pair of slacks, carrying her saxophone.

Gus frowned at the saxophone in her hand. "Why did you bring that?"

"I figured we'd just head to the lounge after this and I'd have it handy."

Gus supposed it wouldn't hurt to drag a saxophone along. She glanced up and down the road. The pear tree was at the end of the village common, away from the shops and skaters. No one was around. She gestured toward the fence. "Okay, now let's be quiet."

As they hopped over the fence, the partridge poked its head out from under a shrub, the light catching the suspicion in its beady black eyes.

"*Peep!*"

"Shush." Gus put her finger to her lips. "Don't tell anyone we're here."

"*Squawk!*" The partridge darted out, and Gus jumped back.

Ivy held her saxophone up in front of her. "That thing is dangerous."

The bird ran a circle around them. Its feathers were falling out, some drifting up in the air and others dropping at Gus's feet. Before Gus could get a good look at it, the partridge disappeared back into the shrubbery.

"What happens to a bird that eats hemlock?" Gus asked.

"I have no idea. Wouldn't they die?"

"Maybe it depends on how much they eat. Maybe only a little bit makes them sick. Vicky must have had a good amount in her food, I suppose." Gus was even more determined to poke around under the tree. She pushed her way into the shrubs behind the tree, figuring that if Comfort or Joy were growing hemlock, it would be in the back section hidden by the tree and shrubs where no one could see.

"Come on over here and let's see what else is growing." They got down on their hands and knees and started poking around. Gus ignored the scratching of the branches on her skin as she poked through clover, buttercups, and even some thorny raspberry bushes. Nothing she found resembled the lacy white flowers of poison hemlock that she'd seen on the internet.

"I don't see anything. Did you say it looks like Queen Anne's lace?" Ivy asked after a few minutes.

"Yes, small white flowers. You might think it's a weed."

"Ouch!" Ivy squealed.

"Shhh… what happened?"

"The partridge pecked me."

Gus turned to see Ivy sitting there holding her elbow, a look of concern on her face. "I hope it can't transmit poison with its beak."

The partridge was sitting behind Ivy, its bedraggled feathers fluffed out. One wing feather hung off at an odd angle. Something was very odd about that bird. "Wait a minute. This bird—"

"Hold it right there! What do you two thieves think you are you doing!" Comfort and Joy pushed their way through the shrubs. Comfort was holding a large box.

"We were just looking for my saxophone reed. I dropped it!" Ivy blurted out, holding up the saxophone case as evidence. Gus looked at her out of the corner of her eye. Surely, she could've come up with something better. She'd need more tutelage before becoming a cop.

Judging by the skeptical looks on their faces, Comfort and Joy weren't buying the reed excuse. "You were spying on us."

Gus stood and brushed dirt off her pants. "Well, not exactly spying. But I think it's mighty suspicious that you are the only people here that have live plants and Vicky was murdered with fresh hemlock." Sometimes the best way to get a confession was to confront the killer bluntly. Of course when Gus usually did this, she had a gun. But now, even as her hand hovered over her right hip, she realized she had no gun. She wasn't in her official capacity. She was simply a tourist jazz piano player on vacation.

"What are you talking about?" Comfort asked.

"She's really nosy. I don't like her," Joy said.

Comfort nodded. "Yeah. I think we better get rid of them."

Ivy's sharp intake of breath indicated her alarm. Gus was alarmed too but also felt a ray of vindication that she had guessed the killer correctly. Still, it was unsettling that they'd killed before, and if Comfort wanted to "get rid of them," she might not stop at killing again. Gus would have to come up with a plan to outmaneuver them, but she wanted answers first.

"Not so fast. What's in the box?" Gus asked.

Comfort pulled the box closer to her chest as if protecting it. "Nothing."

What could possibly be in there? Surely, she wouldn't have more hemlock, would she? And why would she need a fresh batch if she could grow it right here? Something didn't make sense, but that box—and especially the way Comfort clutched it—certainly was suspicious. Gus reached out for the box. "Then you won't mind me looking in there."

Comfort jerked back. "We most certainly will."

Gus lurched forward, grabbing on to the edge. "If you've got nothing to hide, then show me!"

"Get away!" Comfort pulled the box out of Gus's grasp. Gus lurched forward and grabbed more of the box. Comfort tugged back, Gus pulled, and finally the box flew out of both their grasps.

It landed with a thud on the ground and tumbled over. The flaps holding the box shut burst open, and a beautiful brown partridge flew out.

The bird flapped its wings and looked over its

shoulder at them as if admonishing them for dropping the box.

The partridge under the shrub screeched and flapped around. *Wait a minute.* Now that Gus could see the old partridge next to the new one, she realized the birds weren't that much alike. "Exactly what is going on here?"

Comfort and Joy sighed in unison.

"Fine. We might as well tell her," Joy said.

Comfort picked up the original partridge and started petting it, sending feathers flying everywhere. "Our partridge died."

At Gus's raised-brow look, Joy hastened to add, "Not because of anything we did. It was simply old."

Comfort nodded. "And the village couldn't go without a partridge under the pear tree, so we took this peahen and dressed it up like a partridge." She plucked off a feather for proof. Gus could see that the bird was shaped similarly, but the feathers were different colors. They had glued on partridge feathers to make it look like a partridge.

"We figured no one can really get a close look at the bird, and it hides under the shrubs, so this would be a good fix just until we could get a new partridge." Joy picked up the new bird and petted it lovingly then kissed the top of its tiny head. "Here's your new home.

I hope you like it." She placed the bird down and watched as it checked out the area.

"See," Comfort said indignantly. "We treat our birds very well."

The partridge cooed and looked back at them as if in agreement then scurried under a bush, turned around, and peered out at them with its shiny dark eyes.

"What will happen to this bird?" Ivy pointed to the peahen that Comfort cradled in her arms.

"Oh, we'll put her back in the pen at our place. We run a bird sanctuary for injured birds."

"But this still doesn't prove you didn't grow hemlock or kill Vicky. In fact, you had even more of a reason to kill her. She took a big interest in the birds, so she probably discovered that you were having the peahen pose as a partridge," Gus said.

"And you mentioned you were going to *get rid of* us. That sounds like killer talk," Ivy added.

Comfort looked confused. "Huh? Oh, that? I just meant to get you out of here so you wouldn't see us switching birds. You thought we were going to kill you? We're not killers, and we certainly don't grow hemlock here."

"Yeah. It's poisonous and would kill the birds!" Joy added.

She did have a point. The peahen was fine. It wasn't

losing feathers because of poison. Maybe birds were immune to hemlock? But if their story was true, it also explained why they'd been acting so cagey and why Comfort had been so upset when Gus tried to jump over the fence and get into the shrubbery area before. And Vicky didn't like them, so how could they possibly poison her?

"Well, if it wasn't you, then who else would grow the hemlock here?" Ivy demanded.

But Gus already had an idea. Images of fresh mistletoe bubbled up in her mind. Someone else had motive, means, and opportunity. "I think I know—"

Someone said, "I knew it was just a matter of time before you figured it out. Maybe you should have stayed back in Mystic Notch instead of playing sheriff up here. Because now you won't be getting a chance to go back home."

The voice came from behind Comfort and Joy. Gus peered around them to see Mary Dunn. In one hand, she held a rope attached to an old-fashioned wooden sled. In the other, she had a gun, and it was pointed directly at them.

CHAPTER 11

"*M*ary?" Joy's gaze wavered between the gun in Mary's hand and her face. "What is going on?"

Mary rolled her eyes. "Do I have to spell it out?"

"She's the killer," Ivy said.

"That's right, and now that you all know, I'm afraid it's silent night for all of you," Mary said.

"You grew the hemlock right along with the mistletoe." Gus again wished for her gun, but of course she didn't have it. She'd not seen a need to bring it on vacation. Her investigatory skills must have been on vacation, too, she thought, as she remembered the fresh mistletoe in Mary's office. Mary would have had to grow that somewhere.

"Yep. I have a great system set up. Grow lights on

timers. Automated watering system. Temperatures above seventy-five degrees Fahrenheit. Classic Christmas tunes."

"But why?" Comfort clutched the peahen closer.

Mary gestured for them to move farther back into the darkness of the shrubs. Away from the street, where someone might notice what was going on and save them. Not that that was likely. No one came down to this end at night anyway.

Gus edged back slowly, as did everyone else.

"Belinda told me she ran into Vicky coming out of Steven Nicholson's office. I was sure she was bringing some kind of lawsuit against the town, and I couldn't let that happen, now could I?" Mary gestured with the gun, and they all inched back again.

"How did you do it?" Gus figured she might as well get a full confession. She had a plan brewing to get them out of this, and Mary might clam up afterward.

Mary chuckled. "I simply put the hemlock in her breakfast. I knew she picked up the egg sandwich from Good Tidings every morning, so I simply slipped some hemlock in when I dropped off Belinda. Everyone was so busy in the kitchen at that time no one even noticed. Easy peasy. Can you believe it doesn't take very much to kill someone? I was able to put in the right amount, and Vicky apparently never tasted it."

"Clever." Gus was busy calculating whether or not she could disarm Mary before she got a shot off. Disarming her would be risky. The gun pointed right at Joy, who looked terrified. Gus couldn't take the chance that Mary would hit her.

"Yeah. Wasn't it?" Mary seemed pleased with herself. "Then when you came into my office to say you thought it was Wanda and Kevin, I figured they would make the perfect fall guys. Of course I knew Wanda didn't have any hemlock on hand, so I stashed a potted plant near her garage. Hopefully, Detective Winters will find it and put two and two together."

Comfort and Joy gasped. "You're setting them up?"

"Yeah, everyone knows they were having an affair, and anyone who had spent even ten minutes with Vicky would easily see why the husband would want to get rid of her." Mary frowned at Gus and jabbed the gun in her direction. "But then when I saw you on the street, and you said they were denying it and Wanda doesn't even grow fresh herbs, I knew you wouldn't give up. So I dropped the hint about the pear tree and ran home to get my gun. I knew you would run right over to nose around."

"Boy, she sure did." Joy gave Gus an angry glare, as if this were all her fault.

"Okay, enough small talk. Get back further." Mary

gestured and stepped forward, tugging the sled behind her.

They edged backward. Now they were totally hidden behind the drooping branches of the pear tree and the shrubs behind it.

"What's your plan now?" Gus asked. "You can't just shoot us. You have no way to dispose of the bodies."

"No? I think I do." Mary nodded in the direction of the pond on the other side of the bushes. "Those swans a-swimming won't mind if I slide you right in."

So *that* was why she'd brought the sled. Gus glanced over her shoulder. Through a break in the shrubs, she could barely make out the swans gliding on the section of the lake that the water circulators kept from freezing. That end was dark, but on the other end of the lake, skaters whirled under bright lights. The skaters were too far away. No one would see Mary with the sled over by the swans, and the bright lights made it harder for them to see out to the darker side of the pond.

A lone snowman stood beyond the shrub. Gus imagined that she saw a malicious sparkle in his coal eyes, as if he couldn't wait for Mary to turn them into human ice cubes.

"So, you're going to shoot us all and then use the

sled to bring our bodies over and dump us in the water? I'd rethink that. You're outnumbered here." Gus got ready to pounce on Mary as soon as she cocked the hammer. Ideally, Gus could take her down before she got a shot off. If Mary could fire a shot, Gus hoped her aim wasn't that good.

"Yes. You first." Mary aimed at Gus. Darn! Gus was hoping she would aim at someone else so she could jump on her, but with the gun pointing right at her, that wasn't the smartest move. *Now what?*

Gus heard a click as Mary cocked the hammer. "Bye-bye."

Gus's mind whirled. Mary was pointing at the middle of her chest, so if Gus lunged sideways fast enough maybe she could dodge the bullet or even get it in the arm. She hoped she would be mobile enough to take Mary down afterward before she could turn the gun on the others.

But before Mary had a chance to fire, Ivy let out a yell and whipped the saxophone case at Mary.

Clang!

Bam!

The case hit Mary in the chest. The gun went off, shooting a pear down from the tree.

Gus jumped on Mary and pinned her to the ground

just as Detectives Winters and Noel came rushing from the other side of the tree.

Winters looked at Gus and shook her head. "I see you're still resorting to overly dramatic measures to capture the killer."

CHAPTER 12

*L*ater that evening, Gus sat at the bar in the North Pole Lounge. The soothing ambiance with its dark colors, soft acoustics, and twinkling white lights was a welcome contrast to the stressful scene with Mary behind the pear tree.

"…And then Sheriff Chance tackled her, and we swooped in and made the arrest." Detective Winters twirled the stem of the cherry in her Shirley Temple and smiled at Gus. "I always knew you had the makings of a good cop."

Gus frowned. "You did? You always said I'd end up reading meters."

"That was just to push you to do better." Winters sipped her drink. "It worked too."

"She's a hero." Yule's eyes shone with worship as he looked at Gus over the sugar-coated rim of his frothy pink drink.

Gus took a deep breath. The last thing she wanted was for Yule to start fixating on her. He was already sitting too close. She scooted her chair away from him. "Ivy is really the hero. She beaned Mary with her saxophone."

"It's a good thing it didn't get dented." Ivy, who had been holding the instrument in her lap, looked it over for the fiftieth time.

"That thing makes a good weapon. I'll have to remember that when I get back to Mystic Notch," Gus joked then turned to Winters. "Seriously, though, you should consider adding Ivy to the police force."

Winters smiled. "Actually, I am. When she graduates from the police academy, we'll have a place for her."

Ivy blushed. "Thanks. To both of you."

Both Gus and Winters waved the thanks away.

"You earned it," Winters said. "Mary gave us a full confession. She's been very naughty and will be going away for a long time. Thanks for your help on the case."

"You're welcome." Gus smiled at Winters. Her old

teacher wasn't so bad after all. Winters had even confessed that she'd made things fair by ensuring Gus knew that Vicky had been poisoned with hemlock. She knew Gus wouldn't be able to come by that information and figured she couldn't resist investigating. Gus suspected it might have been some sort of test, but Winters had said one could never have enough help trying to catch a killer.

"I know it's difficult to catch a killer when you don't have the benefit of police support behind you. Maybe you should go easier on your sister now that you know how hard it is," Winters said.

Gus jerked her gaze from her drink, meeting Winters's blue eyes. "How did you know about Willa?"

Noel rolled his eyes. "She knows everything. It's almost like she sees you when you're sleeping."

"I'd like to see you while you're sleeping," Yule whispered to Gus.

Gus moved farther away from him.

Ivy shot Yule a stop-acting-like-a-creeper look and said to Gus, "It's true. She knows if you've been bad or good."

"Okay, this is getting weird." Gus finished off her Cosmo and stood. "Come on, let's go play some jazz."

A feeling of satisfaction washed over Gus as she sat

behind the black baby grand. Finally, she was getting to do what she'd come here for: play the piano.

Of course, it didn't hurt that she'd been able to prove to her old teacher that she really was a success at law enforcement…though that last part about Winters knowing about Willa and that bit about seeing her while she was sleeping was a bit disturbing. Even so, she made a mental note that she better be good for goodness's sake.

****

I hope you enjoyed this Christmas Novella! It features Gus from the Mystic Notch Series. You can check out the full length books in that series here:

Mystic Notch

Find out about my latest books and how to get discounts on them by signing up at:

https://leighanndobbscozymysteries.gr8.com

If you want to receive a text message alert on your cell

phone for new releases , text COZYMYSTERY to 88202 (sorry, this only works for US cell phones!)

Join my VIP readers group on Facebook
https://www.facebook.com/groups/ldobbsreaders

Cozy Mysteries

Mystic Notch

Cat Cozy Mystery Series

* * *

Ghostly Paws

A Spirited Tail

A Mew To A Kill

Paws and Effect

Probable Paws

Whisker of a Doubt

Wrong Side of the Claw

Oyster Cove Guesthouse

Cat Cozy Mystery Series

***

A Twist in the Tail

A Whisker in the Dark

Kate Diamond Mystery Adventures

***

Hidden Agemda (Book 1)

Ancient Hiss Story (Book 2)

Heist Society (Book 3)

Silver Hollow

Paranormal Cozy Mystery Series

***

A Spell of Trouble (Book 1)

Spell Disaster (Book 2)

Nothing to Croak About (Book 3)

Cry Wolf (Book 4)

Shear Magic (Book 5)

Mooseamuck Island

Cozy Mystery Series

* * *

A Zen For Murder

A Crabby Killer

A Treacherous Treasure

Blackmoore Sisters

Cozy Mystery Series

* * *

Dead Wrong

Dead & Buried

Dead Tide

Buried Secrets

Deadly Intentions

A Grave Mistake

Spell Found

Fatal Fortune

Hidden Secrets

Lexy Baker

Cozy Mystery Series

* * *

Lexy Baker Cozy Mystery Series Boxed Set Vol 1 (Books 1-4)

Or buy the books separately:

Killer Cupcakes

Dying For Danish

Murder, Money and Marzipan

3 Bodies and a Biscotti

Brownies, Bodies & Bad Guys

Bake, Battle & Roll

Wedded Blintz

Scones, Skulls & Scams

Ice Cream Murder

Mummified Meringues

Brutal Brulee (Novella)

No Scone Unturned

Cream Puff Killer

Never Say Pie

Lady Katherine Regency Mysteries

***

An Invitation to Murder (Book 1)

The Baffling Burglaries of Bath (Book 2)

Murder at the Ice Ball (Book 3)

A Murderous Affair (Book 4)

Hazel Martin Historical Mystery Series

***

Murder at Lowry House (book 1)

Murder by Misunderstanding (book 2)

Sam Mason Mysteries

(As L. A. Dobbs)

***

Telling Lies (Book 1)

Keeping Secrets (Book 2)

Exposing Truths (Book 3)

Betraying Trust (Book 4)

Killing Dreams (Book 5)

Rockford Security Series

***

Deadly Betrayal (Book 1)

Fatal Games (Book 2)

Treacherous Seduction (Book 3)

Calculating Desires (Book 4)

Wicked Deception (Book 5)

Criminal Intentions (Book 6)

Romantic Comedy

***

Corporate Chaos Series

In Over Her Head (book 1)

Can't Stand the Heat (book 2)

What Goes Around Comes Around (book 3)

Careful What You Wish For (4)

Contemporary Romance

***

Reluctant Romance

Sweet Romance (Written As Annie Dobbs)

Firefly Inn Series

***

Another Chance (Book 1)

Another Wish (Book 2)

Hometown Hearts Series

***

No Getting Over You (Book 1)

A Change of Heart (Book 2)

Sweet Mountain Billionaires

***

Jaded Billionaire (Book 1)

A Billion Reasons Not To Fall In Love (Book 2)

***

Sweetrock Sweet and Spicy Cowboy Romance

Some Like It Hot

Too Close For Comfort

―――

Regency Romance

* * *

Scandals and Spies Series:

Kissing The Enemy

Deceiving the Duke

Tempting the Rival

Charming the Spy

Pursuing the Traitor

Captivating the Captain

The Unexpected Series:

An Unexpected Proposal

An Unexpected Passion

Dobbs Fancytales:

Dobbs Fancytales Boxed Set Collection

Western Historical Romance

***

Goldwater Creek Mail Order Brides:

Faith

American Mail Order Brides Series:

Chevonne: Bride of Oklahoma

Magical Romance with a Touch of Mystery

***

Something Magical

Curiously Enchanted

ABOUT THE AUTHOR

USA Today best-selling Author, Leighann Dobbs, has had a passion for reading since she was old enough to hold a book, but she didn't put pen to paper until much later in life. After a twenty-year career as a software engineer, with a few side trips into selling antiques and making jewelry, she realized you can't make a living reading books, so she tried her hand at writing them and discovered she had a passion for that, too! She lives in New Hampshire with her husband, Bruce, their trusty Chihuahua mix, Mojo, and beautiful rescue cat, Kitty.

Find out about her latest books and how to get discounts on them by signing up at:

https://leighanndobbscozymysteries.gr8.com

If you want to receive a text message alert on your cell phone for new releases , text COZYMYSTERY to 88202 (sorry, this only works for US cell phones!)

Join the VIP readers group on Facebook

https://www.facebook.com/groups/ldobbsreaders

Made in United States
North Haven, CT
05 March 2023

33616018R00065